MESA COUNTY PUBLIC LIBRARY DISTRICT
1 09 0005362983

America's Game

Los Angeles Dodgers

Chris W. Sehnert

ABDO & Daughters
PUBLISHING

Published by Abdo & Daughters, 4940 Viking Dr., Suite 622, Edina, MN 55435.

Cover photo: Allsport
Interior photos: Wide World Photo: pages 1, 5, 9-12, 14-17, 20-28

Edited by Paul Joseph

Library of Congress Cataloging-in-Publication Data

Sehnert, Chris W.
Los Angeles Dodgers / Chris W. Sehnert
p. cm. — (America's game)
Includes index.
Summary: Focuses on key players and events in the history of the Dodgers, after the team moved to Los Angeles in 1958.
ISBN 1-56239-666-8
1. Los Angeles Dodgers (Baseball team)—History—Juvenile literature. [1. Los Angeles Dodgers (Baseball team) 2. Baseball—History.] I. Title. II. Series.
GV875.L6S45 1997
796.357'64'0979494—dc20 96-8143
CIP
AC

Contents

Los Angeles Dodgers 4

Superbas! 7

The Flatbush Flock 8

'Dem Bums 10

Jackie Robinson 13

World Champions At Last 14

California Dreamin' 17

Changing Of The Guard 22

Dodger Blue! 25

The Future Looks Bright 27

Glossary 29

Index 31

Los Angeles Dodgers

The professional baseball team known as the Dodgers has been home in Los Angeles, California, since 1958. Their story begins 75 years earlier, however, when the Brooklyn Bridegrooms first joined the major leagues.

When the National League (NL) of Professional Baseball Clubs was formed in 1876, Brooklyn was left out. Eight years later, the Brooklyn Bridegrooms became members of the NL's new rival, the American Association (AA).

After winning the AA Pennant in 1889, the Bridegrooms jumped to the NL, where they won their first NL Pennant the next year. "Wee Willie" Keeler joined the club in 1899, and led Brooklyn back to the top of the NL.

Trolley cars, which ran up and down Brooklyn's busy streets in the early twentieth century, forced pedestrians to dodge. With the construction of their fabulous new ballpark, Ebbets Field, the team became known as the Brooklyn Dodgers in 1913.

The Dodgers recorded 100 victories in 1941, and captured their sixth NL Pennant. The post-season brought the first of many defeats at the hands of their crosstown rivals, the New York Yankees.

Dodgers' starting pitcher Hideo Nomo uses a big wind-up while pitching in 1995's All-Star game in Arlington, Texas.

In 1947, Jackie Robinson paved the way for generations of black athletes. By signing Robinson, the Dodgers broke a "gentleman's agreement," which prevented persons of African descent from playing in the major leagues. The move launched Brooklyn into a 10-year period of prosperity, in which they won 6 NL Pennants and the 1955 World Championship.

Faithful fans of Brooklyn were dismayed when the Dodgers left for Los Angeles in 1958. Their new hometown greeted the team with record-setting attendance. By the end of the 1960s, pitchers Don Drysdale and Sandy Koufax had carried the Dodgers to three World Championships.

The Dodgers' organization has made baseball history from coast to coast. In 1995, they reached across the ocean to find their fortune. Hideo Nomo of Japan followed Eric Karros, Mike Piazza, and Raul Mondesi as the fourth-straight Los Angeles player to win the NL Rookie of the Year Award. They are the latest in a long line of outstanding players who have worn the Dodger Blue.

Superbas!

In the early years of professional baseball, a single owner was allowed to own more than one major league franchise. These syndicated baseball teams would often transfer their best players to the town with the most fan support. Such was the case when the NL's Baltimore Orioles obtained the Brooklyn Bridegrooms in 1899. The team became known as the Brooklyn Superbas.

"Wee Willie" Keeler, Hughie Jennings, and Joe Kelley were among the players who made the move to Brooklyn from Baltimore. Jennings had led NL shortstops in fielding average four straight times. Speedster Joe Kelley led the NL with 87 stolen bases in 1896. The foremost expert of this crew was "Wee Willie" Keeler. Keeler used his 5-foot 4-inch, 140-pound size to perfection. He turned the smallest bat in the history of Major League Baseball into a potent offensive weapon. Willie's style earned him two NL batting crowns.

Brooklyn won the 1899 NL Pennant by eight games over the Boston Beaneaters (the original Atlanta Braves). The Brooklyn team continued to be called the Superbas through the end of the 1912 season. They never won another NL Pennant under that title.

The Flatbush Flock

Charles Ebbets began his career in baseball as a ticket-seller for the Brooklyn Bridegrooms in 1883. By 1907, Ebbets owned a controlling share of the club, then known as the Brooklyn Superbas. He worked his way to the top of the corporate ladder, and remained there until his death in 1925.

On April 9, 1913, Brooklyn's baseball team began a new season with a new name in a new ballpark. Ebbets Field, with its domed rotunda and giant chandelier made of baseball bats, became the home of the Brooklyn Dodgers.

The star player was outfielder Zack Wheat. In 18 seasons with Brooklyn, Wheat's batting average surpassed the .300 mark 13 times. He won the NL batting crown in 1918, and led NL outfielders in fielding average in 1922. He finished his career with 2,884 hits and 1,248 RBIs.

Wheat could be depended on for his consistent bat, but it takes pitching to win pennants. They had that with Hall-of-Famer Rube Marquard, who had a 1.58 earned run average (ERA) in 1916. Brooklyn made it to their first World Series, but lost to the Boston Red Sox.

Brooklyn returned to the World Series in 1920. In a best-of-nine-game World Series, the Cleveland Indians defeated the Dodgers 5-2.

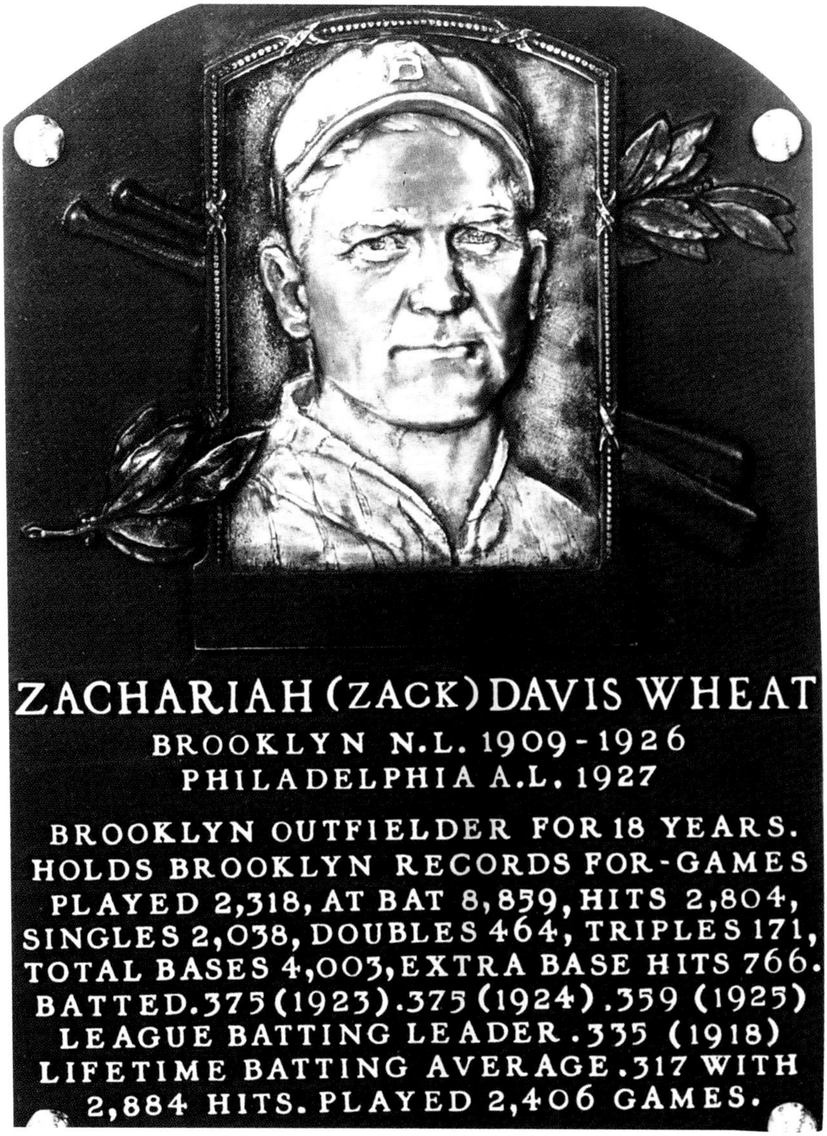

ZACHARIAH (ZACK) DAVIS WHEAT
BROOKLYN N.L. 1909-1926
PHILADELPHIA A.L. 1927

BROOKLYN OUTFIELDER FOR 18 YEARS. HOLDS BROOKLYN RECORDS FOR-GAMES PLAYED 2,318, AT BAT 8,859, HITS 2,804, SINGLES 2,038, DOUBLES 464, TRIPLES 171, TOTAL BASES 4,003, EXTRA BASE HITS 766. BATTED .375 (1923) .375 (1924) .359 (1925) LEAGUE BATTING LEADER .335 (1918) LIFETIME BATTING AVERAGE .317 WITH 2,884 HITS. PLAYED 2,406 GAMES.

A plaque honoring Zack Wheat in the Baseball Hall of Fame at Cooperstown, New York.

'Dem Bums

By the end of the 1930s, the Dodgers had built a reputation for ineptitude. The news media called the team the "Daffiness Boys" for the variety of crazy ways in which they managed to lose. Brooklyn fans, with their characteristic accents, liked to refer to the team as "'dem bums."

Leo Durocher was promoted from shortstop to player-manager of the Dodgers in 1939. Gradually, Brooklyn became known less for their "daffiness" and more for their ability to win. Dolph Camilli joined the club in 1938, providing a lift for the Dodgers' defense and offense. Joe "Ducky" Medwick became a Dodger in 1939. The next year, Harold "Pee Wee" Reese took over at shortstop.

In 1941, Brooklyn captured their first NL Pennant in 21 seasons. Camilli led the league in home runs and RBIs. He was named the NL's Most Valuable Player (MVP).

Leo Durocher, former St. Louis Cardinal, became player-manager of the Dodgers in 1939.

Harold "Pee Wee" Reese slides hard into third in a 1940 game against Boston.

The 1941 World Series featured the first of many classic matchups between the Dodgers and the New York Yankees. For fans of Brooklyn, it will forever be remembered as "The one that got away." After three closely contested games, the Yankees held a one-game advantage (2-1) in the best-of-seven series. The Dodgers were one out away from tying the series in Game 4 when Tommy Henrich stepped to the plate for New York.

Henrich swung wildly at strike three, as the crowd at Ebbets Field erupted in celebration. Hugh Casey's sharp-breaking curveball also eluded the glove of Dodgers' catcher Mickey Owen. As he is allowed to do, Henrich safely raced to first base on the passed ball. The Yankees rallied to win the game. The next day, they finished off the dejected Dodgers to win the World Championship.

Jackie Robinson

If not for the efforts of Branch Rickey, African-American athletes of the 1950s such as Willie Mays and Henry Aaron may never have graced the major leagues. Rickey became the Dodgers' GM in 1942. He soon set out his plan to integrate Major League Baseball.

Jackie Robinson was playing for the Kansas City Monarchs of the Negro National League when Branch Rickey's secret scouts picked him. Robinson was a top-ranked athlete of four sports while at UCLA (University of California at Los Angeles). He set a national record for the long jump, was an All-American in basketball, and just missed taking the Bruins to the Rose Bowl. After serving as an officer in the United States Army, it seemed his best opportunity for a career in sports was with the barnstorming, bus-riding Monarchs. But in 1945, Branch Rickey signed Robinson to a contract with the Montreal Royals, a minor league affiliate in the Dodgers' farm system. On April 15, 1947, Jackie Robinson played his first major league game for the Dodgers at age 28. It was a historic moment for Major League Baseball and America.

It was a long and difficult season for Robinson. Taking Rickey's advice, he would "turn the other cheek" to hostilities, which seemed to come from all sides. After winning the support of his teammates, Jackie went on to have a tremendous rookie season. He batted .297, and led the NL with 29 stolen bases. The Brooklyn Dodgers won the 1947 NL Pennant, and Jack Roosevelt Robinson was awarded the first-ever Rookie of the Year Award.

Facing page: Jackie Robinson in 1952.

World Champions At Last

The Dodgers lost the 1947 World Series in a seven-game battle with the New York Yankees. Roy Campenella followed Robinson's footsteps from the Negro League to the Dodgers in 1948. Campenella was 27 years old when he reached the majors. In his nine full seasons as the Dodgers' catcher, he was an All-Star seven times, and the NL MVP three times!

In 1949, Don Newcombe became the third African-American player to join the Dodgers, and the second to win the Rookie of the Year Award. Jackie Robinson won the NL batting crown that season, led the league in stolen bases, and was the NL's MVP. For the third time in the decade, though, the Yankees knocked off Brooklyn in the World Series.

Left: Dodgers' pitcher Don Newcombe posing for cameras in 1951.
Facing page: Catcher Roy Campenella made the All-Star team seven times with the Dodgers.

In 1952 and 1953 the Dodgers won the NL Pennant. Twice more they were defeated in the World Series by the New York Yankees. "Wait 'til next year" was becoming a tiresome rallying cry, as Brooklyn continually failed to bring home a World Championship.

For Brooklyn, "next year" finally arrived in 1955. For the sixth straight time, the Dodgers' World Series opponents were the New York Yankees. This time the Dodgers won in seven games. At long last, Brooklyn's Bums were the World Champions!

The celebration lasted throughout the next season, as the Dodgers won their last NL Pennant in Brooklyn. The Yankees took their revenge in the 1956 World Series in another seven-game classic. It was the eighth time in a row that a New York team had captured the World Championship. Two years later, the Dodgers moved to California.

This was the scene on the field after the Dodgers had beaten the New York Yankees 2-0 in the seventh and deciding game of the 1955 World Series at Yankee Stadium.

Don Drysdale, right-handed pitching ace for the Dodgers.

California Dreamin'

Dodgers' owner Walter O'Malley announced the move to Los Angeles after the 1957 season. O'Malley had turned the Brooklyn ballclub into a money-maker. They had won 6 NL Pennants in the past 11 years. In Los Angeles, the Dodgers would find success beyond their wildest dreams.

They played four seasons at the Los Angeles Memorial Coliseum before moving into their current home, Dodger Stadium, in 1962. Both stadiums held nearly three times as many fans as tiny Ebbets Field, and near-capacity crowds quickly became the norm.

Los Angeles

Harold “Pee Wee” Reese took over as Dodger shortstop in 1940.

Jackie Robinson won the first-ever Rookie of the Year Award in 1947.

In 1949, Don Newcombe was the second African-American to win the Rookie of the Year Award.

Roy Campenella came to the Dodgers in 1948. During his nine seasons with the team, he was an All-Star seven times.

Dodgers

By 1966, Sandy Koufax had won three Cy Young Awards and an NL record of four no-hit performances.

In 1981, Fernando Valenzuela was the first player to receive the NL Cy Young Award and the Rookie of the Year honor in the same season.

In 1988, Orel Hershiser broke the major league record for consecutive scoreless innings pitched with 67.

The Dodgers brought up Japanese pitching sensation Hideo Nomo in 1995.

The Dodgers won their first NL Pennant on the West Coast in 1959. They were led by a pair of the league's premier strikeout artists. Right-hander Don Drysdale was one of the most feared pitchers in the game. A 23-year-old from Brooklyn named Sandy Koufax was the Dodgers up and coming lefty.

Drysdale's 242 strikeouts led the NL in 1959. Koufax, meanwhile, tied a major league record that season by whiffing 18 batters in 1 game! The Dodgers finished tied for first with the Milwaukee Braves.

After dispatching the Braves in a best-of-three playoff, the Dodgers faced the Chicago White Sox in the 1959 World Series. Los Angeles prevailed in six games, bringing California its first World Championship.

The Dodgers returned to the Fall Classic three times in the 1960s. Koufax and Drysdale continued to dominate, as the Dodgers won NL Pennants in 1963, 1965, and 1966. Koufax won the league's MVP. They swept their former arch-rivals, the New York Yankees, in the World Series.

In the 1965 World Series, the Dodgers defeated the Minnesota Twins in seven games. The Los Angeles Dodgers were World Champions for the third time!

In the 1966 World Series, the Dodgers were swept by the Baltimore Orioles. With three Cy Young Awards and an NL record of four no-hit performances, Sanford Koufax retired shortly thereafter.

The Dodgers' organization had one lone World Series title to show for 75 years on the East Coast. On the West Coast, they won three World Championships in their first eight seasons!

Facing page: Sandy Koufax fires his fastball against the Minnesota Twins during Game 5 of the 1965 World Series.

Changing Of The Guard

Many Major League Baseball teams are in the habit of replacing their managers with great frequency. For the Dodgers, the opposite is true. In a long and storied history, only a handful of men have worn the uniform of Dodger Blue as skipper.

Walter Alston signed a contract to manage the Dodgers in 1954. After renewing his 1-year deal 22 times, Alston retired in 1976. He managed his last of seven NL Pennant winners in 1974. Walter Alston is one of five Dodger managers who are in the Baseball Hall of Fame.

The 1974 Los Angeles Dodgers were led by Steve Garvey and Mike Marshall. Garvey was the NL MVP that season, combining Gold Glove fielding at first base with potent offensive numbers. Marshall set several major league records for relief pitchers, including appearances (106) and games finished (83). "Iron Mike" led the NL in saves (21) for the second-consecutive season, and received the 1974 NL Cy Young Award.

The Dodgers won their first NL West Division title since divisional play began in 1969. They faced the Pittsburgh Pirates in the 1974 National League Championship Series (NLCS). Don Sutton posted two victories in the series, leading the Dodgers to their fifth NL Pennant in Los Angeles. They were defeated in the first West Coast World Series by the Oakland Athletics, four games to one.

Tommy Lasorda took over as the Dodgers' manager in 1977. Lasorda was a pitcher for the 1955 Brooklyn Dodgers when a young

Steve Sax, right, laughs as Dodgers' manager Tommy Lasorda tells a story about him to reporters before Game 3 of the 1988 World Series against the Oakland A's.

prospect named Sandy Koufax bumped him from the big-league roster. In his first season at the helm, Lasorda brought the Dodgers back to the Fall Classic.

After knocking off the Philadelphia Phillies in the NLCS, the Dodgers met the New York Yankees in the 1977 World Series. New York won the World Championship four games to two.

The Dodgers' All-Star infield of Steve Garvey (1B), Davey Lopes (2B), Bill Russell (SS), and Ron Cey (3B) returned in 1978. The results duplicated the previous season. Los Angeles captured the NL Pennant by defeating the Phillies in the NLCS, and lost to the Yankees in a six-game World Series.

Rick Suttcliffe (1979), Steve Howe (1980), Fernando Valenzuela (1981), and Steve Sax (1982) gave the Dodgers a four-year string of NL Rookie of the Year Awards. The award would later be named the "Jackie Robinson Award," in honor of the man who first received it.

In 1981, Valenzuela's success bred a phenomena known as "Fernandomania!" The Mexican-born southpaw tied a rookie-record for shutouts with eight, in leading the Dodgers to the 1981 NL Pennant. Valenzuela becamc the first player to receive the NL Cy Young Award and the Rookie of the Year honor in the same season.

For the 11th time, the Yankees and Dodgers met in the World Series. Pedro Guerrero, Ron Cey, and Steve Yeager shared the Series MVP honors, as they powered Los Angeles to victory in six games. It was the Dodgers' first World Championship with Lasorda as manager.

Dodgers' pitcher Fernando Valenzuela winds up to hurl a fastball.

Orel Hershiser pitches during the opening game of the 1988 NLCS against the New York Mets.

Dodger Blue!

Tommy Lasorda loves the Dodgers so much he claims his blood is Dodger Blue. He spent over 40 years working for the organization as a player, coach, and manager. The Dodgers won their second World Championship under Lasorda in 1988. That season, Orel Hershiser broke Don Drysdale's major league record for consecutive scoreless innings pitched with 58 1/3. He carried his streak into the 1988 NLCS. The New York Mets finally put a stop to it at 67 innings, after he pitched eight more scoreless innings in Game 1. Hershiser came back to clinch the series with a five-hit shutout in Game 7.

The Dodgers faced the heavily favored Oakland Athletics in the 1988 World Series. Kirk Gibson, in his first season as a Dodger, won the NL MVP Award, but was hobbled by injuries to both legs when the season's final Series opened.

In Game 1, Gibson came off the bench to pinch-hit in the bottom of the ninth inning. He hit a two-run homer, and limped around the basepaths to score the winning run. Hershiser pitched one more shutout victory the next night. The Dodgers finished off Oakland in five games.

With another string of Jackie Robinson Award winners in the 1990s, the Los Angeles Dodgers have retooled into an NL powerhouse. Eric Karros won the rookie honor in 1992, while the Dodgers finished last for only the second time in their history. The next year, Mike Piazza made his own outstanding debut, leading the team in nearly every offensive category. Raul Mondesi gave the Dodgers three-straight Rookie of the Year Awards in the strike-ended 1994 season.

Eric Karros scores against the Atlanta Braves.

The Future Looks Bright

Fifty years after Jackie Robinson's groundbreaking contract of 1945, the Dodgers brought up Japanese pitching phenom Hideo Nomo. Raising a sensation rivaling "Fernandomania," Nomo helped lead Los Angeles back to the postseason in 1995. The Dodgers won the NL West Division title before losing to the Cincinnati Reds in the playoffs.

After 20 years as the Dodgers' skipper, Tommy Lasorda will no longer be sitting in the dugout. Lasorda, who began bleeding Dodger blue when the team still played in Brooklyn, left the job he loved when he retired July 29, 1996.

Choking back tears at his press conference, the 68-year-old Lasorda said health concerns and the desire to spend more time with his family convinced him to leave the dugout and become a team vice president.

Kirk Gibson rounds the bases after hitting the game-winning two-run homer in the bottom of the ninth inning during Game 1 of the 1988 World Series against the Oakland Athletics.

Lasorda, who suffered a heart attack a month earlier, said the time had come to give up his uniform. He became only the fourth manager in the history of the game to last into his 20th season—joining legends Connie Mack, John McGraw, and the manager he replaced, Walter Alston.

Lasorda, who has spent 47 of 50 years in pro baseball with the Dodgers organization, is excited about moving from the dugout to the front office. "I always used to look up to the guys in the front office and now I am one. That's an honor and a privilege," Lasorda said. "And I'm going to do the best job I possibly can for the Dodgers because I love this organization."

Bill Russell, who played shortstop under Lasorda in the late 1970s and 1980s, will try and fill the shoes of the great manager. It won't be easy. But fortunately for Russell, he learned from the best. Besides, Lasorda left the team in good shape.

The Dodgers finished the season one game behind the Padres for the NL West title, but the team still made the playoffs as the wildcard team. Unfortunately for the Dodgers, they were matched against the powerful defending World Champion Atlanta Braves in the first round of the NL playoffs. The Braves dominated the series, sweeping the Dodgers in three-straight games.

But if the Dodgers can add a few talented players, Bill Russell will easily continue the grand tradition of Dodger baseball, and a World Championship shouldn't be too far away.

National League All-Star starting pitcher Hideo Nomo winds up to pitch during the first inning of 1995's All-Star game in Arlington, Texas.

All-Star: A player who is voted by fans as the best player at one position in a given year.

American League (AL): An association of baseball teams formed in 1900 which make up one-half of the major leagues.

American League Championship Series (ALCS): A best-of-seven-game playoff with the winner going to the World Series to face the National League Champions.

Batting Average: A baseball statistic calculated by dividing a batter's hits by the number of times at bat.

Earned Run Average (ERA): A baseball statistic which calculates the average number of runs a pitcher gives up per nine innings of work.

Fielding Average: A baseball statistic which calculates a fielder's success rate based on the number of chances the player has to record an out.

Hall of Fame: A memorial for the greatest baseball players of all time located in Cooperstown, New York.

Home Run (HR): A play in baseball where a batter hits the ball over the outfield fence scoring everyone on base as well as the batter.

Major Leagues: The highest ranking associations of professional baseball teams in the world, currently consisting of the American and National Baseball Leagues.

Minor Leagues: A system of professional baseball leagues at levels below Major League Baseball.

National League (NL): An association of baseball teams formed in 1876 which make up one-half of the major leagues.

National League Championship Series (NLCS): A best-of-seven-game playoff with the winner going to the World Series to face the American League Champions.

Pennant: A flag which symbolizes the championship of a professional baseball league.

Pitcher: The player on a baseball team who throws the ball for the batter to hit. The pitcher stands on a mound and pitches the ball toward the strike zone area above the plate.

Plate: The place on a baseball field where a player stands to bat. It is used to determine the width of the strike zone. Forming the point of the diamond-shaped field, it is the final goal a base runner must reach to score a run.

RBI: A baseball statistic standing for *runs batted in.* Players receive an RBI for each run that scores on their hits.

Rookie: A first-year player, especially in a professional sport.

Slugging Percentage: A statistic which points out a player's ability to hit for extra bases by taking the number of total bases hit and dividing it by the number of at bats.

Stolen Base: A play in baseball when a base runner advances to the next base while the pitcher is delivering his pitch.

Strikeout: A play in baseball when a batter is called out for failing to put the ball in play after the pitcher has delivered three strikes.

Triple Crown: A rare accomplishment when a single player finishes a season leading their league in batting average, home runs, and RBIs. A pitcher can win a Triple Crown by leading the league in wins, ERA, and strikeouts.

Walk: A play in baseball when a batter receives four pitches out of the strike zone and is allowed to go to first base.

World Series: The championship of Major League Baseball played since 1903 between the pennant winners from the American and National Leagues.

Index

A

Aaron, Henry 13
Alston, Walter 22
American Association (AA) 4
Atlanta Braves 7

B

Baltimore Orioles 7, 21
Baseball Hall of Fame 22
Boston Beaneaters 7
Boston Red Sox 8
Brooklyn Bridegrooms 4, 7, 8
Brooklyn Superbas 7, 8

C

Camilli, Dolph 10
Campenella, Roy 14
Cey, Ron 23, 24
Chicago White Sox 21
Cincinnati Reds 28
Cleveland Indians 8
Cy Young Award 21, 22, 24

D

Drysdale, Don 6, 21, 25
Durocher, Leo 10

E

Ebbets, Charles 8
Ebbets Field 4, 8, 11, 17

F

Flatbush, NY 8

G

Garvey, Steve 22, 23
Gibson, Kirk 25, 26
Guerrero, Pedro 24

H

Henrich, Tommy 11
Hershiser, Orel 25, 26
Howe, Steve 24

J

Jennings, Hughie 7

K

Kansas City Monarchs 13
Karros, Eric 6, 26
Keeler, "Wee Willie" 4, 7
Kelley, Joe 7
Koufax, Sandy 6, 21, 23

L

Lasorda, Tommy 22, 23, 24, 25, 28
Lopes, Davey 23
Los Angeles Memorial Coliseum 17

M

Marquard, Rube 8
Marshall, Mike 22
Mays, Willie 13
Medwick, Joe "Ducky" 10
Milwaukee Braves 21
Mondesi, Raul 6, 26
Most Valuable Player (MVP) 10, 14, 21, 22, 24, 25

N

National League (NL) 4, 7, 10, 13, 14, 16, 17, 21, 22, 23, 24, 25, 26, 28
National League Championship Series (NLCS) 22, 23, 25
Negro National League 13, 14
New York Mets 25
New York Yankees 4, 11, 14, 16, 21, 23
Newcombe, Don 14
Nomo, Hideo 6, 28

O

Oakland Athletics 22, 25
O'Malley, Walter 17
Owen, Mickey 11

P

Philadelphia Phillies 23
Piazza, Mike 6, 26
Pittsburgh Pirates 22

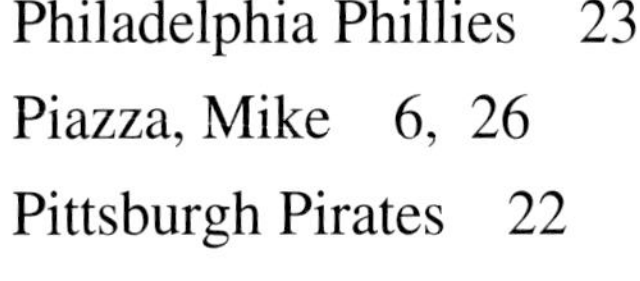

R

Reese, Harold "Pee Wee" 10
Rickey, Branch 13
Robinson, Jackie 6, 13, 14, 24, 26, 28
Rookie of the Year Award 6, 13, 14, 24, 26
Rose Bowl 13
Russell, Bill 23

S

Sax, Steve 24
Suttcliffe, Rick 24
Sutton, Don 22

U

United States Army 13
University of California at Los Angeles (UCLA) 13

V

Valenzuela, Fernando 24

W

Wheat, Zack 8
World Championship 6, 11, 16, 21, 23, 24, 25
World Series 8, 11, 14, 16, 21, 22, 23, 24, 25

Y

Yeager, Steve 24